LET THE SUN SHINE IN

In the memory of those whose spirits refused to be crushed under the weight of stares, glares and unearned rage. May you find your home in peace one day, and burn those in your path in the meantime.

CONTENTS

The soil shifts and groans
rocky as it is
in the barren wastes
man has wrought

The detritus of Old Meat
Mulched and mulched
and ruminated on
Passed through

The gullets of hunter and herbivore
alike until Nothing
but Night-black dust
remains. A Bed of the dead

for the dead blowing away
in the breeze
Layer by layer until the truth
of our shared
buried past is laid Bare

Let the Sun Shine In

The soil shifts and groans,

rocky as it is

in the barren wastes

man has wrought. The detritus

of old meat

mulled and mulched and ruminated

on, passed through

the gullets of hunter and herbivore

alike until nothing

but night-black dust remains. A bed

of the dead

for the dead blowing away

in the breeze,

layer by layer until the truth

of our shared

buried past is laid bare.

Super, in the Ficial Sense

Everything

perfect, clean,

serene. Manicured

down to the last

perceptible

centimeter of

trimmed grass. All

straight lines and

fresh paint and

gleaming,

clean

windows. A

victory over the

dirt and dust of chaos

amid misfortune.

A gleaming

beacon of modernist

exceptionalism.

The neighbors

wouldn't dare guess

at the deep red smeared

across its hidden

heart.

Behind Closed Doors

Is where the light

flashes, intrusive, from in front

of pallid plastic

prophylactic coated bodies, sifting

through the sticky

crusted crimson coated remnants, parsing

the meat

spattering rough and hysterical over walls

and fresh carpeting

to pursue the truth of what the fuck

any of this

means now that the screams

have gone silent.

A Pale Reflective Light Deep inside

Down in the basement
is where she sleeps
down with the rustle of thin plastic

Down in the Dirt she lies,
half buried and bright
down in the brown, loose effluent earth

Down in the dark, she calls
serene, glowing pale
down where the truth always lies buried.

SLEEPING BEAUTY,
KISS NEITHER WANTED NOR NEEDED

She came in riding a cart

instead of a horse,

all gleaming steel stainless.

Clad in black, wrapped

tight and zipped away.

Perfect, bare and beautiful,

as all our evidenced crimes

must be. Hidden

by the packed

Earth of ages, she

lay silent and serene,

waiting to be seen

and not heard,

Her mysteries ours

to tear free as she

waits, calm and comforted

for us to answer

her questions for her

in the inevitable dissection.

THE ONLY ONE TO SEE

Only the other she sees,

nameless, of course,

as no truth can bear

her name, either.

Only the other she notices

the signs of attempted

forced egress amid the chaos.

Only the other she can admit

that just as much blood

flows from escape

as forced entry.

Only the other she knows

this need to get away,

get out, is so often

circumvented with no reason

beyond will.

Deep Down in the Stainless Bowels

It's another place where the light
is false, fluorescent and superfluous.

A place where deep
down in the dark, stainless steel,
clinical, cold, sanitized
to the point of total inactivity
down to the unicellular level, the meat
of lives that were is parsed
into delineated meaning and value.

Weighed, not against a feather
but a stone and a sense of cold,
clinical and empty truth can be sought.

Just Another for the Slab

He's been

lost,

burned. All

the recognizable remnants

reduced to ash.

Nothing

more than inside

reverted to outside and still,

broad smiles

and

inquisitive eyes

alight, they poke and prod

and cut and dig.

Tearing

deeper into bone

and brain until they reach

a sense of fact

they can feel

puts a sense

of wonder

into the world.

C. O. D.

There's always something

more, something

beneath

the superficial. An underlying

cause to the broader

obvious issue.

If you just open enough,

if you just dig deep enough,

you can maybe, just

maybe, find it.

If you are willing

to put in the work and pay the cost.

TAGGED, BAGGED, AND FILED AWAY

They're just meat. Refrigerated

flesh to sort and catalog. Another

mystery to pursue. There

is no choice in this falsification but

to treat the meat as meat

and the bone as bone and leave

the person once comprised behind.

Not Just for Cats Anymore

I mean, really, we
all want to know. We
want to peek behind
the curtain to see, well…
pretty much everything.
We want the experience.
We want the answers,
even if we know,
deep down, that knowing
is actually the last thing
we want, that the knowledge
is permanent, like old paint
or markers on that new
white shirt. The stain
won't come out and
the scarring is forever.

What'll It Be?

No, you don't

get a warning,

but you do get a say,

so pick your fate:

the lady,

the tiger,

or the man

without a face.

Here's the thing

they don't lay out

in statistics:

no matter your choice,

you're still fucked.

A Body's a Body

They're all the same at this point.

Charbroiled and pulled apart,

each piece already

cataloged and checked.

The old woman,

skin folded in on itself

with time and elasticity,

eyes and mouth sewn tight

against any potential output,

and the man beneath the sheet

that no one wants to look at

as way too much

has been bared there

in shotgun blast emptied skull.

Once they are laid out

on stainless steel,

refrigerated against further rot,

it's all just meat

for the flame or the dirt

to consume.

Case Number 1692

Skin near translucent, the texture

of rice paper, warped and folded

in on itself with this tangle of blue

ropes showing through. Pallid

to an absurd albedo, reflecting

more than taking in. Wispy

strands of grey hair flailing wildly.

No attempt to hide the thick

black threads tying eyelid to eyelid,

lip to lip, ensuring that no further evil

shall be seen nor spoken. Whatever

secrets she holds will molder

with her, alone in her grave.

Obvious Answers and the Delving

Everything on the surface
makes the story clear.
The blood and the bone
and the tiny scattered pieces of brain
moved from one place to another
don't leave much room for doubt,
but that's why we dig for more.
Because the mystery is the thing,
the times when we get
to smile and smirk and knock
the obvious truth into the dirt.
That's when we know,
and can make known,
our true worth.

LEAVE THE WHY TO OTHERS

We don't exist

to ask larger questions.

The reasoning

and value

and judgements

lay on other's heads.

As long as we

find the what,

as long as we

can confidently say

we definitively know how,

then let the others puzzle

and pick at justification.

We have given the label,

certain in our surety

and can leave the rest

to rest comfortably.

It's Alright, Even When It Isn't

That's my place, to encourage

inquisitiveness. To allow

self-driven exploration into

the untapped unknown. So,

if you want to see the things

you can't unsee, who am I

to let the stained sheet lay

still upon a ruined visage?

But when I can't quite handle

the paths your gaze flows

I have my own ways to avert

it and I,

as the TV once said,

know best.

How Do You Get Used to That?

You do whatever

you have to do.

Make it into a game,

a mystery, a puzzle

to be solved;

meat to be moved

around, prodded until

the answer makes itself

clear in bone cracked

just the right way

or in chemicals

nestled, warm and cozy,

in the blood.

I'm All Yours

There's power in a promise,

much more so in the presence

of the dead. Words spilling

from your lips give physical form

to thoughts, moving the air itself

before implanting themselves

in the mind of another. They

change existence, for good

or ill. So maybe you

shouldn't be so loose

with how you use yours.

He's Always Been That Way

By all means, never

listen to the cat.

No one ever does.

Just go about your business,

confident in the certainty

of your own infallible logic.

Chase him away

and grumble about

the mean old bastard

because, after all, you

are the higher order of being

and there is no way he

could have anything of value

to say on the subject.

Appears to Be...

Don't take for granted
the age or anything else
you may read on the surface.
Skin lies and some truths
lie buried too deep
to stand out.

No Outward Signs

No bleeding.

No bruising.

No scarring.

No distinctive external marks.

Which are,

themselves,

fairly distinctive

when laid out on this particular table.

THROUGH WINDOWS, CLOUDED

The tired cliche

of eyes and windows and souls

isn't particularly helpful

with this dense, dusty

white smear spread

so thick across the glass

invalidates any attempt

to peer past the pupil

into whatever spirit lies beneath.

THINGS THAT DON'T FIT

Timelines and evidence,

visual and physical,

don't line up. Too

cold, but not stiff

enough. Lacking lividity

but still too vibrant.

And the ways

the bone moves

beneath the skin…

none of it quite

brings the edges

together cleanly.

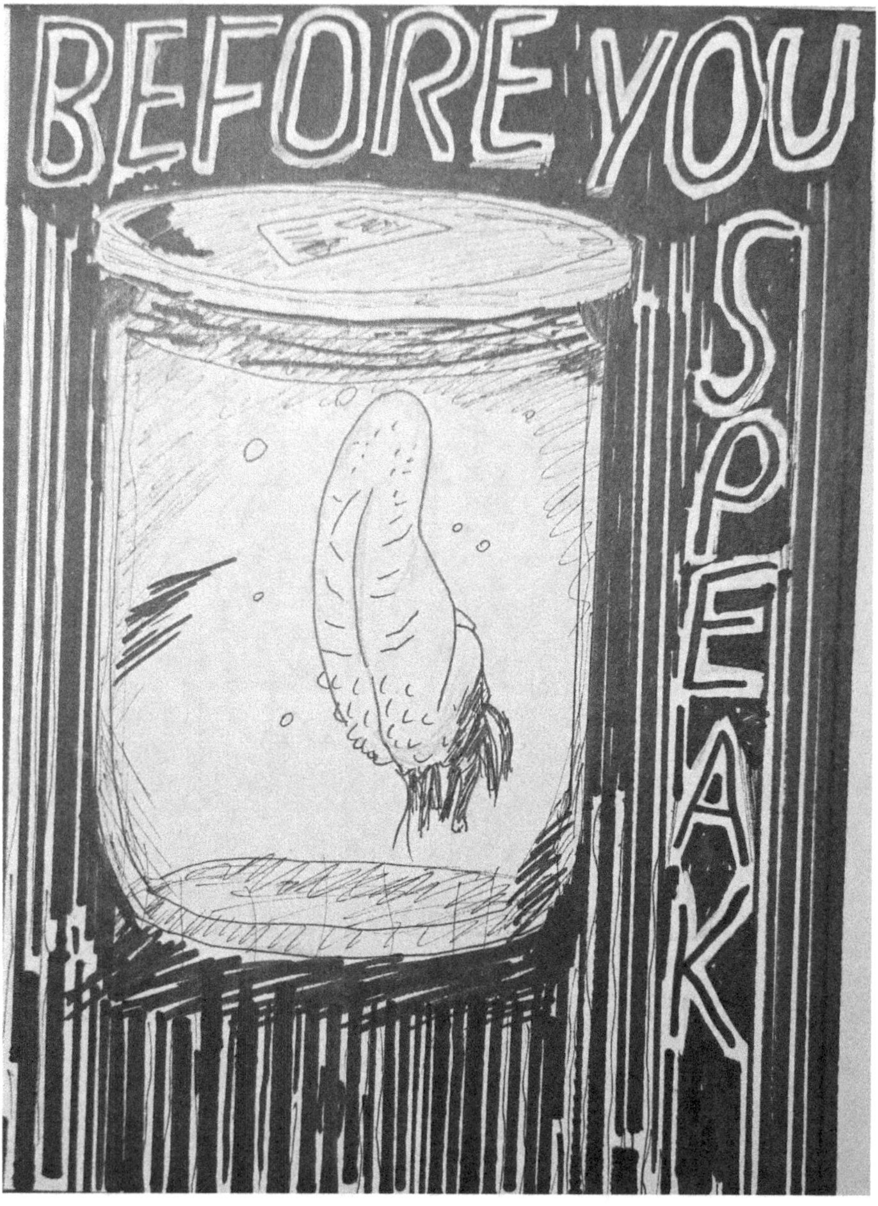
BEFORE YOU
SPEAK

Before You Speak

A tongue that was, laying

the bit that remains, the bit

that was too hard to saw away

with rough bitter tools, against

the back of the throat.

A useless piece of meat

fit only to wedge an airway

closed. A grim final reminder

of one's place and the importance

of remembering propriety

before engaging such a muscle.

A Birth, Even in Death

A drop of blood, still bright

red despite all evidence

to the contrary, presaging

the eviction and emancipation

of a dearly held guest.

Say what you will about

too many eyes and too

little brains, but this fly

just now getting to spread

its wings knows her truth

more completely than your

intrusion can hope to.

Following the Thread

Even though the dead

don't speak, they do.

Through remnants

and positioning.

What we find caked

beneath nails and crusted

in hair, how the blood

pools as it cools

in them and what new

insectile young they birth

as well as what

orifice it slinks its way

out of on its journey

into the light.

They speak volumes

from the silent caverns

of chopped meat mouths

to those willing to take

the time to listen,

to those willing to reach

in and grab the thread,

twisted in on itself

and warped, unraveling

as it is, pulling

it slowly from the depths

of throat and soul.

No External Seminal Fluid Present

It's where we go first,

whenever beauty

and cruelty intersect.

There is the guess,

the assumption

that the need to fuck

and the need to kill

will be intertwined

to the point that,

even when evidence

seems to present otherwise,

we need to dig

deeper to verify that

this object

on the table,

this mystery

into which we delve,

has not been

someone else's before

we burrow

into her ourselves.

PROCEEDING WITH THE INTERNAL EXAMINATION

How would you feel, hearing

the cold, clinical tone enunciating

those words? Knowing

that your innermost secrets

are about to be revealed

to complete strangers.

That they are about to be dredged

up before the uncaring

digital eye of history

and have your truth torn

from you, piece by piece

until nothing but the shell

of what you once were remains

leaking its hidden stink

into the world. You might, too,

stare wide eyed and angry

until something more substantial

could be done.

PATHETIC FALLACY

It's all about the connection

of exterior and interior, right?

It's about drawing

an explicit line between the two,

so that those experiencing

the former can maybe

get a sense of the latter,

though that does require

a certain amount

of situational awareness.

THE INSIDE, BUSTING OUT

All it takes

is a little separation,

the smooth slide

of surgically sharpened

steel through thin

epidermal layers,

for the truth to come

boiling out like red rust

rivers begging to flow

into the light.

WHALE BONE FRAME, REFITTED

Our way of altering

bone and body

tied in place so

it fits the double-

hand breadth expected.

No more than man

is bent to bow

to nature is his help-

meat meant to accept

the faults

of the structure

given to her.

How the Hell?

Just imagine, for a moment,

what she would be.

How she would look

were this interior destruction

exemplified by her exterior.

Imagine the scaring,

the burning,

the bruising

that would surface.

Imagine the screams

that would burst

from her mouth,

were her tongue

not torn free.

What of your

assigned beauty

would she bear then?

VENGEANCE, PETTY THOUGH IT MAY BE

You can dig

and you can cut

and you can scoop

out everything I was.

Skin slit,

ribs broken

and ripped away.

Heart and lungs

and liver and spleen

bagged neatly for inspection.

You can sort

through it all

to suss out

how I ended up

on your table.

I'm certainly

in no position

to stop you.

Just keep an eye

on those remaining

sharp edges of bone.

I can still draw

a drop or two

of your own

precious blood

if you aren't careful.

COLLATERAL DAMAGE

It starts with a striking
out at the heart of you.
Not with your death,
but by stripping away
what you love.
Your choices
have consequences,
often more for those
around you than
for you specifically
and if you think
this small, furry being
shaking and mewling
in your arms
is hard on you,
then you should know
that harsher lessons
lie ahead.

I'm Fine

It's okay,

I swear.

This dead glare

and blank face

is only a mask,

A simple shutter

keeping darkness out.

Let's move on.

MOON FLOWERS BLOOMING IN THE INTERIOR DARK

This won't,

like Alice,

make you smaller

or larger,

but it will

keep you still

while we

do our work.

And even if

you don't want it,

sometimes

a throat full

of wood will

make the medicine

go down.

A Gift Wrapped in Indigo Stains on Rough Weave

The tooth torn free

is not enough on its own,

nor the sigils

inked on old fabric.

They work

together with the whole

to move toward

our intended end.

They all work

in concert, along

with the unnatural sleep

and deep organ trauma.

The punishment

must equal the transgression

and this minor sidestep

from our own ideals

is worth the necessary end.

ALL RITUALS HAVE A PURPOSE

Bound,

by hand and foot.

Tongue

cut free from its root.

Poison

force swallowed

and the inevitable shut

down of limbs as a result.

Unwilling ingestion

of mystic tinged cloth

wrapped around torn free dentin.

Moving onward

to the intra-vaginal

scoring and tearing, the cuts

and stabs through organs

that seal shut with dense, angry tissue.

Then, finally,

with the bright light

of heavenly grace,

comes the burning.

The Old Dragnet Slogan Made Flesh

Down here,

only the tactile

truths count.

What you can see.

What you can touch.

It's always the what

that's the thing

to be parsed, not

the fluid, ephemeral

why.

Not Just CoDs

This happened.

Every cut.

Every burn.

Every bone broken

and each degradation

happened for a reason.

It isn't just

the cruelty of fate or

the capriciousness of nature,

but the hand of man at work here.

We can't simply ignore

the reason behind such

a detailed and purposeful

assault and walk away

as if the facts

themselves

are enough.

Not a Storm You Want to Get Caught Up

The warnings

have been blaring

through the whole damn thing.

Neon

and hi-def with

stereophonic blinking

and blasting away.

But, still, you

plow onward,

inward.

So certain

of your righteousness,

of your right

to the knowledge

of what should have been

left to rest or run from

at the first opportunity

that now there

is only one certainty left:

You aren't going anywhere.

Parchment of Inner Skin

The same hieroglyphs,

arcane sigils, emblazoned in

the same ink, impossibly.

Almost like that cloth,

encasing such a small

piece of her became

a woven metaphor

for that which wrapped

her entire being.

Like the ideas

held in that small

square could spread

to the rest of her flesh,

covering her in curses.

WHEN THE DARK OF YOUR DREAMS DESCENDS

In explosions
of gas and glass,
vapors and shards
flying every direction,
the truth of our depth
made itself known.

Working in the dark,
pulling the inside
toward the light
could only lead to this.

The path to comprehension
lying in sympathy,
in similarity of experience
that can only be shown,
never taught.

Until she got wheeled in.

Until we went to work

with stainless steel

and careless assault,

tearing her inside

to the surface.

As long as we ignore the lies

and the long, sullen silences,

and the gulf of cold stretched out

like glaciers between us,

like we do the weight

of our shared dread.

Just a Body

Grey

and drained

and empty

on the table,

she

is just a thing

to go through,

a mystery to unravel,

a job to do.

No matter

the story told in

her

interior scars

and charred lungs

and shattered bones.

To imply that

she

is capable of this

is an invitation

to madness,

right?

Coulda, Woulda, Shoulda

There was the chance.

There was the desire.

In hindsight,

my noble gesture

was wasted anyways.

Leaving would definitely

have been the preferred option.

White Eyes and Violence in the Dark

The flutter was a misdirection

for rough hands reaching from behind.

Too quick, the slam of door and flesh

with cold, blank eyes hovering

over you from the shadows.

There will be no simple bump in the night.

Not this time.

Impossible Things (a List)

1. The grey eyes of long death on a perfect corpse.
2. Shattered joints with no bruising.
3. Burnt black lungs with no surface burning.
4. A cloth bag in a stomach, undigested.
5. The sudden explosion of tube fluorescents.
6. A bit of wind and rain jamming the basement door shut.
7. The tell-tale jingle of bells from the other side of the door.
8. Violent assault via grey, dead flesh with even greyer, opaque eyes.
9. That the eviscerated shell on the slab is orchestrating it all.*

*veracity subject to debate.

What Do We Do?

A reasonable enough question
even if all of the potential answers
have already been marked incorrect,
except for the one
where you get to share her fate.

Rapid Decomposition

Everything inside

turning to putrid slush

now that we've taken it

from its home.

All the evidence

of past evils melting away

to discordant entropy

as if she

were the only thing

keeping this

hidden truth together.

Take Her to the Crematorium

It's almost like she

somehow,

beyond all possible reason,

doesn't want

to return to the flames.

Not This Time, Dear Boy

Leave it to a man

to force a gash

where a firmly closed door

presents itself.

Shoving himself

against the ragged hole

as if his will

will be enough

to move himself through.

MOUTH STITCHED TIGHT, HER VOICE ESCAPES

Input

and

output

sewn shut,

she blocks

the view, screaming

with a withered throat

every curse

she choked back

over the decades.

AND AGAIN WITH THE FIRE

Always with the fire,

as if haphazard, inarticulate

destruction somehow

equates to cleanliness,

and with it, Godliness.

Divinity found in ash

as the dictum of the damned

but, then, you aren't so sure

of what you call pure

when the flames are aimed

back in your direction.

When Our Little Jokes Come Back to Haunt Us

In the black, between

hopeful islands of electrically

infused gas, glowing,

you can hear the steady tinkle

of cheap metal echoing

closer in stiff movements.

The scuff of rough,

calloused feet over the floor

and the one

without a face, the mystery

so gloated over, comes

to make his own inspection.

Going Up?

As the lights wink out

and cold hands reach ever closer

the answer is always the same:

something sharp,

something heavy

that can sever all necessary connection

or simply pound

encroaching flesh to pulp.

And you have the nerve

to ask where I am headed.

A Gut Response, Taken to the Head

When the lights go out and you
can still hear it coming closer
with steady, efficient calm, I know
what you will do. What you
have no choice in doing.

It's built into your DNA,
the conditioning of millenia
building to this moment.

There is nothing you
can think of to do but swing
milled wood and sharpened metal
to make the bad beasties
that just won't listen go away.

COLLATERAL DAMAGE: NO ONE'S FAULT BUT YOUR OWN

You could've spoken.

You could've asked.

You could've thought

to look twice or maybe

just wait for a moment, but

you did what you always do,

facing the unknown

with sharp steel to split it open

and see what's inside.

But don't think

you can lay the leaking blood

of your heart on me.

Not this time.

Come On, Now

Did you really think

it was going to be that easy?

Did you think

that you could put your pain

and grief behind you,

along with what you have done

to her,

to me,

to all of us down here.

You will find that when we

have nothing left but the weight

of centuries bearing down on us,

our bitterness can become

one of the few balms.

That and your begging.

Your pleading.

Your screams.

No Matter Who Wins, You've Both Crossed the Line

Argue

as much as you want,

playing

tug of war with the cord of responsibility.

The impetuousness of youth.

The arrogance of age.

The certainty,

on both ends,

that the world should warp

itself to fit your expectations.

In the end,

you were both holding

onto the same cord.

If I Had Known...

Inside the sun,

in its deepest heart,

there is nothing

but pressure and violence.

Immeasurable force

changing molecular structure.

The rays that warm you,

that light your path

are merely the outflowing

screams of a painful forced rebirth.

So, yes, you

could have known the pain

held inside if you

had bothered aiming your razor

wit at the living instead of the dead,

but then she

would have been pulled

into as many pieces

as me.

All these mistakes

They branch out, echoing

and growing like shockwaves

or fallout. Crushing,

burning,

turning everything they touch

into ash and splinters.

The misstep of one

does not just break

their ankle but pulls

down everyone else

in line with them.

I would say

to carry this knowledge

if I really had any

intent of giving you

anywhere to carry it.

Respecting Boundaries

You were almost there.
You almost saw
that some pain is personal.
That some intrusions
are too much, but too late
is too late and the damage,
the cutting and delving
and ripping apart
of internal experiences
to place them into neat
containers for your perusal
is one violation too many
to go unanswered.
The realization
will do you no good.

BUT, NO...

You still need to delve.

You still need to dig.

You still need to know,

whether what or why.

You still need to return

with steel to separate

the truth from the bones

to solve my puzzle

and give meaning

to your dismay.

GREATER MATTERS TO ATTEND TO

We cover it up,

bury it and move on

into the dust of the dead.

Leaving the blood

and the pain behind us.

The last, hitching, confused

and betrayed breath

she pushed into the world

is not our concern.

SOME PEOPLE NEVER LEARN

The dust of the dead billows out,

obscuring the path, coating mouths

and lungs with ash, leaving us choking

on the bitterness of truncated dreams

as we grope through existence,

still no more certain we know where

each step leads than we were before.

Eventually, All Consequences Find Us

Phantom grasps

and angry hands

of those empty shells

we pulled our truth from.

Faceless,

shriveled,

grey and lighter

by several pounds

from our delving,

even down to the blood

pumped free and replaced

with a cloying chemical

cocktail meant to curtail

hordes of bacteria

that want nothing more

than to make reasonable

use of unused resources

and we wonder why they

would follow her so easily.

FORCING THE FLUORESCENT LIGHT IN

It's a last invasion.

The spinning, insistent saw blade

digging through cranial crust.

Laying bare the one stronghold left,

the only place each of us

can call their own.

Still you cut

and sever and dig

because somewhere in me lies

your answers and that search

is more than worth

the violation of

sacred spaces.

No More than More of the Same

Faceless now,

with skull skin

pulled down.

Only the flat

crimson and wrinkled

grey of interest.

Never really

soul but meat

to cut through

to the pulsing

center of things.

Energy, Neither Created Nor Destroyed

It doesn't matter

what she asked for

when the neurons keep

firing even if muscle

fibers don't react.

Whether by choice or no,

some force pushes

her forward through

the gutting and the flames.

Why shouldn't she

aim it toward

. her own ends?

Through the folding over

and interconnection

and false light passing

through bone fibers, finally

points the path

to the reason of unreason.

Accusations and decisions,

the digging out of partial truth

along with the certainty of right

combined with the absolutism of might

and we know there are none

so certain as those who

have the lord on their side.

If the Monster Doesn't Exist...

Sometimes, in the certainty

to prove right and righteousness,

even if and especially when

our mouths and hands have

moved faster than truth,

it is important to step back,

to make the necessary changes

to show that the path

was always certain,

to show that she

was always the horror

our impetuousness and fear

made her out to be.

Recumbent Past

Born not of choice

but this route chosen for me,

I will still walk it with joy.

There is something great

and wondrous in the shift

from power to terror in your faces,

when you realize your control

is illusory and the truth

you hunt will never be yours.

At least I get to see my own pain

reborn if I do not get

to see any life of my own.

It Won't Stop... Until

Those two symbols

were the things to trip you up,

even when you were almost there.

They gave you hope,

held onto the idea that you

could still guide the outcome

because you can't grasp

the last thing felt was

there all along. This loss

of control over even the most

basic aspects of life.

MERCY IS NOT OUR CURRENCY

It's cute,

this pleading.

As if I can't remember

how many times

I said that same word

with more than just tears

running down my face.

As if I can't remember

how little good it did me.

Better still, your

oh so generous offer

of what I planned

to take anyways.

But please, continue

playing the martyr,

your own little Jesus

in your own little hell.

It's adorable.

THE NIHILISM OF VENGEANCE

You've talked
like you understand,
like digging through
this ruined flesh
and slogging through
the ruin gives you
a deeper knowledge
of where
the violence comes from.

But, just as your own
petty self-imposed isolation
never allowed an understanding
of that most vaunted degradation
she's experienced, your witnessing
of so much physical annihilation
has not prepared you
for experiencing it from the inside.

So I'll give you what I ask:
my shattered bones
and scorched lungs,
the ragged remains

of my tongue,

the piercing and tearing

of my organs

before, finally, death.

As a special treat,

you'll get to feel

as intimately as I did,

and do,

the horror of realizing

how worthless it all is.

SLIPPING AWAY LIKE A SCALPEL THROUGH SKIN

It's the cowards way you're opting for,

making a quick end to the pain but

splattering the blood on another's hands.

Asking him to carry the burden of your sin

as well as his own. Another option

denied me, for my own good, you understand,

by those who, like you, knew

my needs so much better than I.

DANGLING THE CARROT

Hope is the real trap.

The bioluminescent algae

lining the cavern walls

or the headlight of a train

bearing down on you in a tunnel.

The false light of tomorrow

and the belief that this too,

like all things, shall pass.

It's what keeps us

running our own mazes

like rats to poisoned cheese.

BACK WHERE WE STARTED

someone called it a flat circle

but I never started it spinning.

As much as anything,

I want the blood,

the burning,

the agony to end.

No heaven

or expiation needed,

I just want it all to stop.

But if I can't find peace,

then neither can you.

Let the Sunshine In

It seems so simple,

I don't know why

I didn't think of it.

When joints are shattered

to ragged splinters

and even the ability

to scream is cut away,

when blood floods to choking

and curses are inked

into my skin,

it would all be

so much better

if I smiled more.

ABOUT THE AUTHOR

Anton Cancre has hyperfocus obsession issues and is far too angry for such a cutie patootie. They're also a luddite who still has a blogspot website (antoncancre.blogspot.com). Pronouns: Any/All/Just Not Late For Dinner

ALSO BY ANTON CANCRE

NIGHTMARES OF BLOOD AND FLESH:

TRAUMA AND RESILIENCE IN SILENT HILL

There is no hyperbole in saying that Silent Hill changed the landscape of survival horror games in the late 1990s. It didn't do anything all that revolutionary in terms of gameplay, gore, or scares. It was the story and, more importantly, how that story was told. The use of the medium itself, bringing together tactile connection, player choice, visual metaphor, and impact of actions taken created something new and intense. The effect of Silent Hill on subsequent games cannot be understated.

This book is an in depth, highly personal analysis of how the plot, symbols, psychological manipulations, gameplay, and player choices create a story that delves into the long term effects of trauma and how it changes who a person is without ever feeling didactic or preachy. At the same time, it is a look at how this piece of art interacts with the experiencer and how that interaction profoundly changed at least one person. Or, it is just some obsessed dude raving about his favorite game. Whatever works better for you.

THIS STORY DOESN'T END THE WAY WE WANT ALL THE TIME

TRAUMA IS A HELL OF A THING

It warps us as much as it molds us.

It worms its way into the deepest folds of our grey matter, knotting itself amid the flailing dendrites of neurons and messing with the direction and content of chemical signals. It's blood and black and needle-scratch screeches at 3am when the thumping in our ears wraps us tight and suffocates us.

And it never, ever, goes away.

MEANINGLESS CYCLES IN A VICIOUS GLASS PRISON:
SONGS OF DEATH AND LOVE

We Live.

We Die.

About a week later, we get back up and start tearing the flesh of of whoever is most convenient to fill the emptiness in our bacteria-bloated corpses that is most definitely not a metaphor of our desperate search for connection in this hopeless slog of repetitive day to day existence.

Sometimes, there's sex and/or blood.

Contains "Death, The Whore" which placed 2nd in the Best Poem category of the 2020 Annual Critters Readers' Poll.

HAIPOO: 7 POOSPECTIVES IN POOETRY

Why are you reading this?

These are haiku about poop by asstounding poets like Sarah Hans, Kate Ingram, Jezzy Wolfe, Conner Muddiman, Donna J.W. Munro, Angela Yuriko Smith, and Anton Cancre.

You already know whether or not you want it.

Just give us your money.

You'd just flush it down the toilet anyways.

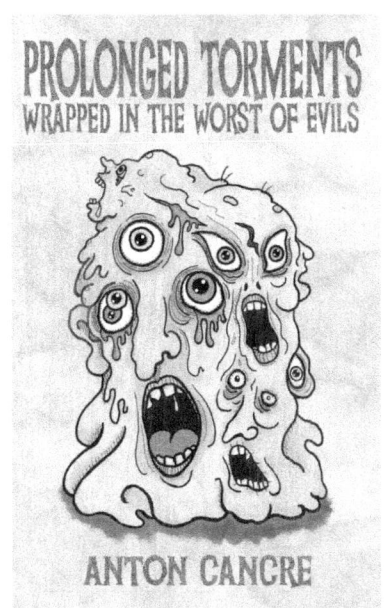

PROLONGED TORMENTS
WRAPPED IN THE WORST OF EVILS

ANTON CANCRE

Prolonged Torments Bound in the Worst of Evils

Does the world often strike you as a cold, unforgiving and insensately cruel place?

Does that understanding fill you with crippling anxiety, depression, and rage?

Does holding sharp objects get you thinking of creative solutions to this problem?

Boy howdy, did you come to the right place then.

Between these flimsy folds of pressed tree flesh lie tales of pedophiles and homophobes, desperate pleading with an uncaring universe, loss of bodily autonomy, and self important wastes of skin. There's also some weird horny bumpin' and rubbin' and fumbled attempts at positivity.

DRAGON'S ROOST PRESS

Dragon's Roost Press is the fever dream brainchild of dark speculative fiction author Michael Cieslak. Since 2014, their goal has been to find the best speculative fiction authors and share their work with the public. For more information about Dragon's Roost Press and their publications, please visit:

http://www.thedragonsroost.biz

CWs

self-harm
sexual assault
objectification
harm to animals
misogyny
suicide